"Delightful . . . Not only for kids, this series is a *must* for educators, parents, and caregivers who want to help children end the cycle of cruelty."

—**Barbara Coloroso,** best-selling author of *The Bully, the Bullied, and the Bystander*

"I love this series. Kids are sure to empathize with the characters and recognize their own power to stop bullying."

—**Dr. Michele Borba,** internationally recognized child expert and author of *The Big Book of Parenting Solutions*

"The well-drawn characters have real problems with . . . credible resolutions. This [series] should find a home in every school library."

—*Kirkus*

"The books stand alone as separate titles, but they're much more effective when utilized together to give a complete view of how the main characters are feeling and the outside events that help shape their roles."

—*School Library Journal*

"An excellent tool for teaching school-age children good mental health techniques to survive and grow beyond bullying."

—*Children's Bookwatch*, **Reviewer's Choice**

"A good discussion starter."

—*Booklist*

"Incredibly insightful . . . a must-own for educators."

—*Imagination Soup*

TOUGH!

A Story About How to Stop Bullying in Schools

by Erin Frankel

illustrated by Paula Heaphy

free spirit
PUBLISHING®

Acknowledgments

Heartfelt thanks to Judy Galbraith, Meg Bratsch, Steven Hauge, Michelle Lee Lagerroos, and Margie Lisovskis at Free Spirit for their expertise, support, and dedication to making the world a better place for children. Special gratitude to Kelsey, Sofia, and Gabriela for their enthusiasm and ideas during the creation of this book. Appreciation to Naomi Drew for her helpful comments. Thanks also to Alvaro, Thomas, Ann, Paul, Ros, Beth, and all our family and friends for their creative insight and encouragement.

Library of Congress Cataloging-in-Publication Data
Frankel, Erin.
  Tough! / by Erin Frankel ; illustrated by Paula Heaphy.
    p. cm. — (Weird series ; bk. 3)
  ISBN 978-1-57542-400-2 (Hardcover)
1. Bullying—Juvenile literature. 2. Bullying in schools—Juvenile literature. 3. Aggressiveness in children—Juvenile literature. I. Heaphy, Paula. II. Title.
  BF637.B85F728 2012
  302.34'3—dc23

                                                                2012006160

ISBN: 978-1-57542-438-5

Free Spirit Publishing does not have control over or assume responsibility for author or third-party websites and their content.

Reading Level Grade 2; Interest Level Ages 5–9;
Fountas & Pinnell Guided Reading Level M

Edited by Meg Bratsch
Cover and interior design by Michelle Lee Lagerroos
Photo of Erin Frankel by Gabriela Cadahia; photo of Paula Heaphy by Travis Huggett

15 14 13 12 11 10 9
Printed in USA
R18860222

Free Spirit Publishing Inc.
6325 Sandburg Road, Suite 100
Minneapolis, MN 55427-3674
(612) 338-2068
help4kids@freespirit.com
freespirit.com

FSC
100%
From well-managed forests
www.fsc.org

Free Spirit offers competitive pricing.
Contact edsales@freespirit.com for pricing information on multiple quantity purchases.

For all children,
young and old, who
have been involved in bullying.
Don't lose sight of who you are.

Know yourself.
Be yourself.

And always listen
to your heart.

What are you staring at?
I'm not the weird one.
My name is Sam and I'm

TOUGH!

She acts weird.

She talks weird.

Someone has
to tell her,
so I do.

Keeping things cool at school is TOUGH,
but I'm pretty good at it. I get lots of practice.

5

It's a **TOUGH** job, but someone has to make the rules. Around here, that's **me**.

If everyone did what **they** wanted, things would be out of control. Believe me, I know.

"Stop! Give it back, Alex!"

7

The way *I* look at it, people need to be **TOUGH**. You know, learn how to take a joke. I did.

If someone doesn't like the way **I** act,
well that's

TOUGH!

"We're playing my way!"

10

Around here, what I say goes.
No one dares to tell me **no**.

"Hey Jayla, go tell Luisa I think her boots are weird."

So what if I'm a little **TOUGH** on Luisa?
The way *I* look at it, she has it easy.
Always getting the right answer.
Always with her friends.
Always smiling.

Well, at least she *used* to smile.

The truth is, I don't have much to smile about anymore either. Things are getting **TOUGH** around here.

People aren't following my rules.

How *do* I think Luisa feels? That's a **TOUGH** question. I try not to think about other people's feelings.

And the harder I try, the more I forget . . .
What it's like to feel sad.
What it's like to be scared.
Or what it's like to really care.

"Sam, why are you being mean to people? Do you want to talk about it?"

17

I'm *not* being mean.
I'm just being

TOUGH!

I act this way to keep things **cool**.
So people won't mess with me.

Do they *really* think I'm **mean?**

Maybe Mr. C. is right.
Maybe I *could* use a little help.
Someone to tell me: "Enough is enough!"
Someone to help me stop acting
so **TOUGH!**

Someone to help me see that being kind can be **cool**.

"You gave Luisa her boots back, Jayla. That was cool."

"Sam, you can either follow the rules or sit out. The choice is yours."

And someone **else** to make the rules.

21

I'm starting to see that when I'm **kind**, people notice.

"Here."

"Thanks."

22

Changing is **TOUGH**, but the more I act like my real self, the easier it gets.

With everyone **standing up** for each other, school seems like a **cooler** place to be.

STOP BULLYING

Of course, I could always find **someone** to pick on if I really wanted to . . .

... but it feels better to have a **friend** instead.

I discovered something **really amazing!**

When I show people I care—
even just a *little* bit—
they show they care back.
Enough *is* enough!
I'm through with being . . .

31

Sam's Notes

It's *tough* work changing my behavior, but being mean all the time is even tougher. Here are some things I've learned:

Taking my anger out on others only makes me angrier.

Out of control is how I felt before someone helped me change.

Unless I change my behavior, I will keep hurting myself and others.

Giving people a chance is a good way to fit in and be cool.

Having real friends feels a lot better than being tough.

Luisa's Notes

I'm glad Sam is giving up her old ways. I know that I'm not *weird*—no matter what anyone says. Here are some other things I learned as a target of bullying:

When everyone joins together to help, things start getting better.

Every person who is picked on needs someone to stand up for him or her.

I think all people deserve to be treated with kindness, including Sam.

Realizing that no one liked her behavior helped Sam change.

Disrespecting others means you are also disrespecting *yourself*.

Jayla's Notes

I found out that things got a lot harder when I didn't *dare* to stand up for myself and Luisa. Now I feel good about the choices I'm making. Here are some things I know for sure:

Deciding to do what I knew was right took courage.

Assisting Sam when she bullied Luisa meant *I* was bullying, too.

Reaching out to Luisa and being her friend was a good choice.

Eliminating bullying is everyone's responsibility—we all have the power to help.

Join Sam's Kindness Club!

Acting tough didn't take away the hurt I felt when people were mean to me. And it didn't help me make friends, because everyone was scared of me. Now, I'm making choices to show I care, and things are finally starting to change for the better.

I think of my words like notes on my guitar. I try to choose the ones that will help others feel good. Want to help? Just put your fingers on the kind notes below to help me play the right chords.

Wow, it sounds great! Remember, the more you practice, the better you'll get.

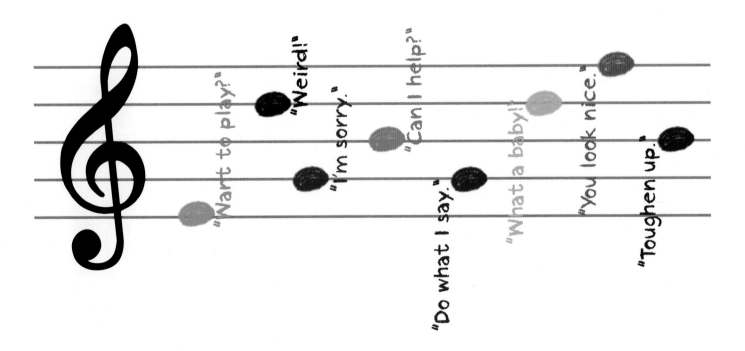

Kindness Club: Picture This

Writing down my thoughts helps me see how my words and actions affect others. Mr. C. calls this activity "reflection." He suggests that I draw my reflections to help me picture what's going on. I could use some help! Grab some paper and let's get started.

1. Draw lines to divide the poster into four equal sections. At the top write: "Picture This."

2. Label the four sections with these questions: "What did I do?" "What did I hope to get by doing it?" "What happened when I did it?" "How can I get what I want without hurting others?"

3. Now read my story again while thinking about these questions.

4. Finally, draw pictures on the poster to describe each of the questions.

Thanks for helping me see what happens when I bully. Are you worried about the way you've been acting toward others lately? Try making your own "Picture This" poster and sharing it with someone you trust.

Kindness Club: Sticking to Caring

I figured no one cared about my feelings, so I chose not to care about others' feelings. But then I found out that people *do* care, and I want to be one of those people. I'm done with being tough and I'm sticking to caring! Want to help me decorate a guitar with stickers?

1. Cut out a large guitar shape from a piece of cardboard. Tape six pieces of string on the cardboard—these are your guitar strings.

2. Cut out heart shapes from a sheet of paper. These are your stickers.

3. In the center of each heart, write words to describe what happens when you stick to caring. *Examples:* I am respectful. I feel happy. I make friends. I'm not lonely.

4. Place tape on the back of your hearts and stick them to your guitar.

5. Pretend to play your new guitar, or hang it in your bedroom. You can also teach a friend how to make one.

Can you think of more activities to do in our Kindness Club? Share them with your classmates and friends. Someone who's kind is *tough* to resist!

A Note to Parents, Teachers, and Other Caring Adults

Every day, millions of children are subjected to bullying in the form of name-calling, threats, insults, belittling, taunting, rumors, and racist slurs—and still more are witnesses to it. Verbal bullying, which can begin as early as preschool, accounts for 70 percent of reported bullying and is often a stepping stone to other types of aggression, including physical, relational, and online bullying. As caring adults, how can we help children feel safe, respected, and confident in who they are? How can we help children who initiate bullying make choices they can feel proud of and end the cycle of violence?

We can start by holding children who bully others accountable for their behavior, while modeling and encouraging positive choices. We can provide kids who are targets of bullying with practical coping tools for positive thinking and confidence building. We can help bystanders explore safe and effective ways to stand up for those who are being bullied. And through stories such as *Tough!*, we can help children develop awareness and perspective-taking skills to help prevent and change bullying behavior. We can help children like Sam understand that by hurting others they are also hurting themselves, and that kindness breeds kindness. We can explore practical strategies to help children act on what they know is right, while providing a trusting environment to support their efforts.

Reflection Questions for *Tough!*

The story told in *Tough!* illustrates a fictional situation, but it is one that many kids will likely relate to even if their experiences have been different. Following are some questions and activities to encourage reflection and dialogue as you read *Tough!* Referring to the main characters by name will help children make connections: *Sam*

Important: **Online bullying (called *cyberbullying*) is a real threat among elementary-age children, given the increased use of smartphones and computers in school and at home. It's also the most difficult type of bullying to stop, because it's less apparent to onlookers. Be sure to include cyberbullying in all of your discussions about bullying with kids.**

initiates the bullying, *Jayla* is a bystander to the bullying, and *Luisa* is the target of the bullying.

Page 1: What do you think of the way Sam introduces herself?

Pages 2–3: What has Sam written and said about Luisa? How does it feel to have someone write or say mean things about you?

Pages 4–7: How does Sam "practice" being a bully? Have you ever witnessed bullying on TV or in movies? How does it make you feel? What is Sam's relationship like with her brother Alex? How do you think this affects Sam's behavior at school? (**Note:** *Children choose to bully others for many reasons. Their motivations are often complex and not easily explained by family relationships, media images, or peer pressure. However, talking about all of these things can help kids understand what might contribute to bullying behavior.*)

Pages 8–9: Why does Sam think people need to be tough? Do you think saying or writing something mean is ever "just a joke"? Why do you think Sam joins in on page 9 when the boys bully Emily (the girl with the violin case)? Have you ever felt pressured to join in bullying someone? What did you do?

Pages 10–11: What does Sam dare Jayla to do on page 11? Why do you think Jayla does what Sam says?

Pages 12–17: How does Sam feel about the way she treats Luisa? What changes are taking place around Sam? What does Sam think about the changes?

Pages 18–19: Do you think Sam is being mean? Does Sam want others to think she is mean? Why or why not?

Pages 20–27: Who helps Sam change her behavior? How does Sam show that she is making positive changes? What does she realize about Emily?

Pages 28–31: What does Sam discover? Do you think she'll continue to bully others?

Overall: Which character in *Tough!* is most like you and why? What would you like to say to this character?

Additional discussion questions, activities, and suggestions for the Weird series are available in the **free Leader's Guide**, which can be downloaded at freespirit.com /leader.

The Weird Series

The Weird series gives readers the opportunity to explore three very different perspectives on bullying: that of a child who is a target of bullying in *Weird!*, that of a bystander to bullying in *Dare!*, and that of a child who initiates bullying in *Tough!* Each book can be used alone or together with the other books in the series to build awareness and engage children in discussions related to bullying and encourage bullying prevention. If you are using the books as a series, consider doing the following activities with young readers.

Series Activity: Chain Reaction

Discuss with children how chain reactions take place throughout each story. Find examples of *negative* chain reactions, and then look for *positive* chain reactions that began as the characters made better choices. For example, when Luisa gave up the things that made her feel special, such as her polka dot boots, Sam felt more powerful and continued to bully her. But when Luisa made a choice to act confident and be herself, Sam felt less powerful and stepped back. Help children define these choices in simple terms and write them down on strips of paper. Give examples of choices in a positive chain reaction: "Acting confident." "Being a friend." "Telling a teacher." "Saying something kind." Invite children to make a paper chain link with their positive choices as a reminder that good choices can start a chain reaction to help end bullying. Children can hang up their paper chains at school or at home.

Series Activity: "Tell to Help" Drawing

Discuss with children how telling adults about a situation in order to get help for themselves or someone else is one of the most important things they can do to help end bullying. Find examples from *Weird!*, *Dare!*, and *Tough!* that show how characters tried to get help by telling an adult, such as Jayla and Will telling Mr. C. about Sam's bullying on page 14 in *Tough!* Ask children to draw a picture of one of these scenes and write "Tell to Help" at the top of the drawing. Have children show their drawings to the class and explain why they think telling helped.

Telling vs. Tattling

Explain to children the important difference between *tattling* on a person for something small (like picking her nose or cutting in line) and *telling* an adult when someone needs help. Ask, "If you were being bullied, you'd want someone to help you, right?"

Series Activity: Round Robin

In small groups, have children retell *Weird!*, *Dare!*, and *Tough!* from the main character's perspective. Each child takes a turn by adding to the story until the story is completed.

Series Activity: What Comes Next?

Weird! Dare! Tough! . . . what comes next? Ask children to imagine and make predictions about what happens to the characters in the next book. Encourage them to consider the main characters: *Luisa*, *Jayla*, and *Sam*, as well as the peripheral characters in the books: *Emily*, *Thomas*, *Patrick*, *Will*, *Mr. C.*, and *Alex*. Then have kids create and present their own book title and storyboard.

About the Author and Illustrator

Erin Frankel has a master's degree in English education and is passionate about parenting, teaching, and writing. She taught ESL in Madrid, Spain, before moving to Pittsburgh, Pennsylvania, with her husband Alvaro and their three daughters, Gabriela, Sofia, and Kelsey. Erin knows firsthand what it feels like to be bullied, and she hopes her stories will help children stay true to who they are and help put an end to bullying. She and her longtime friend and illustrator Paula Heaphy believe in the power of kindness and are grateful to be able to spread that message through their work. In her free time, you'll find Erin hiking in the woods with her family and doggie, Bella, or getting some words down on paper wherever and whenever she can.

Paula Heaphy is a print and pattern designer in the fashion industry. She's an explorer of all artistic mediums from glassblowing to shoemaking, but her biggest love is drawing. She jumped at the chance to illustrate her friend Erin's story, having been bullied herself as a child. As the character of Luisa came to life on paper, Paula felt her path in life suddenly shift into focus. She lives in Brooklyn, New York, where she hopes to use her creativity to light up the hearts of children for years to come.

The Weird Series

by Erin Frankel, illustrated by Paula Heaphy. 48 pp. Ages 5–9.

More Bully Free Kids® Books from Free Spirit

Zach Stands Up
by William Mulcahy,
illustrated by Darren McKee
36 pp. Ages 5–8.

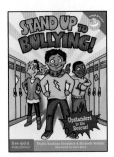

Stand Up to Bullying!
by Phyllis Kaufman Goodstein
and Elizabeth Verdick,
illustrated by Steve Mark
128 pp. Ages 8–13.

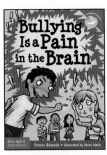

Bullying Is a Pain in the Brain
by Trevor Romain,
illustrated by Steve Mark
112 pp. Ages 8–13.

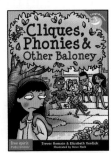

Cliques, Phonies & Other Baloney
by Trevor Romain and Elizabeth Verdick,
illustrated by Steve Mark
112 pp. Ages 8–13.

For pricing information, to place an order, or to request a free catalog, contact:

free spirit PUBLISHING®

6325 Sandburg Road • Suite 100 • Minneapolis, MN 55427-3674 • toll-free 800.735.7323 • local 612.338.2068
fax 612.337.5050 • help4kids@freespirit.com • freespirit.com